Horrible Harry
Cracks the Code

Other Books by Suzy Kline

Horrible Harry Cracks the Code

BY SUZY KLINE
Pictures by Frank Remkiewicz

VIKING

VIKING
Published by Penguin Group
Penguin Young Readers Group,
345 Hudson Street, New York, New York 10014, U.S.A.
Penguin Group (Canada), 90 Eglinton Avenue East, Suite 700, Toronto,
Ontario, Canada M4P 2Y3 (a division of Pearson Penguin Canada Inc.)
Penguin Books Ltd, 80 Strand, London WC2R 0RL, England
Penguin Ireland, 25 St Stephen's Green, Dublin 2, Ireland
(a division of Penguin Books Ltd)
Penguin Group (Australia), 250 Camberwell Road, Camberwell,
Victoria 3124, Australia (a division of Pearson Australia Group Pty Ltd)
Penguin Books India Pvt Ltd, 11 Community Centre, Panchsheel Park,
New Delhi – 110 017, India
Penguin Group (NZ), Cnr Airborne and Rosedale Roads, Albany, Auckland 1310,
New Zealand (a division of Pearson New Zealand Ltd)
Penguin Books (South Africa) (Pty) Ltd, 24 Sturdee Avenue, Rosebank,
Johannesburg 2196, South Africa

Penguin Books Ltd, Registered Offices: 80 Strand, London WC2R 0RL, England

First published in 2007 by Viking, a division of Penguin Young Readers Group

10 9 8 7 6 5 4 3 2 1

Text copyright © Suzy Kline, 2007
Illustrations copyright © Frank Remkiewicz, 2007
All rights reserved

Library of Congress cataloging-in-publication data is available.
ISBN 978-0-670-06200-3

Manufactured in China
Set in New Century Schoolbook

Dedicated with all my love
to my grandson
Holden David Hurtuk,
born August 29, 2006
in Manchester, Connecticut.
You are so blessed to have
Emily and Victor for parents,
and
Mikenna and Saylor for sisters!

Special appreciation to . . .

My grandson Jacob DeAngelis, who first told me about the lucky lunch trays at his Peter Woodbury Elementary School. Thank you so much for all your help! You really inspired this story! I love you!

My granddaughter Mikenna Hurtuk, who asked me to tell her each chapter as I wrote it. Thanks for your interest and questions! I love you!

Pat Bromback, the cafeteria aide at Brookside Elementary School in Ossining, New York, who shared lots of stories with me.

The "Ketchup Lady" at Helen Keller School in Franklin, Massachusetts. I can see how you brighten the children's day, Terry Fenton!

Nasif Mahmud, Sudman Murshed, Himanashu Darji, and Marco Mino at PS 152 in Queens, New York. Thanks for all your help. I loved being at your school for two days.

Jennifer Kim and Kwan Kane, who helped me with Korean good luck.

And a heartfelt thank-you to my husband Rufus, who suggested the deerstalker hat and the Fibonacci sequence. I love you!

And a special appreciation for Dr. Ron Knott's Web site on the Fibonacci numbers, hosted by the Mathematics Department of the University of Surrey, UK. And the Kidshealth.org Web site for a collection of fascinating facts about the Nose Knows.

And especially to the three important people who helped me shape this story—Horrible Harry's talented artist, Frank Remkiewicz; my very sharp editor, Catherine Frank; and my hardworking book designer, Sam Kim.

Contents

Horrible Harry
Cracks the Code

The Ketchup War!

My name is Doug, and I'm in third grade. I write stories about my best friend Harry. He's the guy who loves slimy things, creepy things, and horrible things. He's also the guy who loves being a detective.

He sure messed up his last case, though.

Mary was talking about it at noontime. We were all eating lunch at Room 3B's cafeteria table.

"Harry, I can't believe you thought Miss Mackle was engaged to the music teacher!" she groaned. "You were so sure it was Mr. Marks! Some detective you are!"

Harry stuffed an orange wedge in his mouth and flashed Mary a jack-o'-lantern smile.

"Arrrrrrr aar arrrr," he mumbled.

Song Lee giggled.

Mary ignored Harry. She gently pressed her packet of ketchup four

times to make tiny red dots on her hot dog.

When Sidney squeezed his packet of ketchup, it squirted all over the place. A few drops even landed on Song Lee's pretty white sweater! The pansy on her sleeve was not purple and yellow anymore.

It was red.

Harry immediately took out his orange wedge and dropped it on his blue lunch tray. "Hey, Sid! You got ketchup on Song Lee's sweater! How 'bout saying you're sorry?"

"But it's not my fault," Sid whined. "I can't help it if my ketchup packet doesn't work right."

Song Lee used her spork to scrape off the ketchup. When she finished, we could see a big pink smudge on her sleeve.

"Oh, no! Your favorite sweater is ruined!" Mary groaned.

Harry ripped open one corner of his ketchup packet, leaned toward Sidney, and squeezed it with one mighty push.

Whooooooosh!

Kersplat!

Ketchup landed on Sidney's face.

"Eweeyeee!" Ida said. "Sidney has a bloody nose."

"And bloody teeth!" Mary added.

"But it's not my fault!" Harry replied. "I can't help it if my ketchup packet doesn't work right."

Those were the exact words Sid used!

When Sidney wiped his face with a napkin, he missed some ketchup under his nose. It looked like he had a red mustache!

"Very funny, Harry the Canary!" Sid growled. "Only, I forgot to laugh."

"You'd better not forget to apologize to Song Lee," Harry said. "Or else . . ."

"Or else what?" Sid demanded.

"Or else it's a . . . ketchup war," Harry said, "between you and me!"

"Bring it on, El Tweeto!"

"After you, Sid the Squid!"

Both boys reached for a ketchup packet. Both ripped off one corner.

We all leaned back and got out of the way.

"Fire one!" Sid said, aiming the packet at Harry's face.

Whoooosh!

Harry quickly bowed in prayer. The

ketchup plopped on top of Harry's head. It blended in well with his red hair.

"Fire two!" Harry said as he bobbed up, leaned forward, and squeezed his packet hard at Sid.

Ketchup sprayed along the table.

Most of it landed on Sid's cheek and chin!

Harry ran his fingers through his hair. "Ketchup gel is cool, Sid. Thanks for my new 'do!"

Sidney grabbed his napkin and wiped his face again. He wasn't smil-

ing like Harry. Slowly, he turned and looked at Song Lee. "I'm sorry I got ketchup on you," he said. "I don't like it on me either."

"It was an accident," Song Lee replied with a forgiving smile. "It's okay, Sidney."

"The ketchup war is over!" Harry sang out.

"I'm telling on you boys!" Mary said, raising her hand in the air. "Mrs. Doshi!"

The lunch aide came running over

to our table. "What's going on here?" she said.

"A ketchup war," Mary tattled. "Harry Spooger and Sidney LaFleur are not using their ketchup packets properly. And Song Lee's sweater is stained!"

Mrs. Doshi asked the three ketchup victims to follow her.

Several minutes later, they came

back. Song Lee's sleeve was wet, but you could see the purple-and-yellow pansy. The ketchup was rinsed out.

Sid's face was clean and shiny.

Harry's hair was wet and combed.

Everyone watched Mrs. Doshi walk over to the portable blackboard. She wrote two names in white chalk.

Harry Spooger
Sidney LaFleur

When she returned to our table, she handed Harry and Sidney each a wet sponge.

"You two will wash all the cafeteria tables and all the chairs during lunch recess. The bucket is in the corner." Then she added, "There will be no ketchup packets allowed at this table for the rest of the week. If you want ketchup, I'll give you some from a large bottle."

Harry glared at Mary. "You just cost me a kickball game at noontime. Thanks a lot, Mary!"

"Yeah!" Sid groaned. "Thanks a lot!"

Mary blew up her bangs. "Well, thanks to you we won't have ketchup packets this week."

Harry gritted his teeth. "Listen to me, tattletale. We could have cleaned up the mess ourselves. Tattle on me one more time, Mare, and I'll tattle on you!"

Mary snickered. "That could never happen, Harry Spooger!" she said. "I *always* follow the rules!"

Always? I thought.

It was just a matter of time.

The Biggest Case
Ever in Room 3B

The next morning when we were hanging up our jackets in Room 3B, Harry had a bag under his arm. "Okay, guys, I know why I goofed up my last case," he said.

Mary hung up her wool scarf. "I do too. You're a horrible detective!"

Harry opened his bag. "Nope. I just forgot to wear my detective hat."

"Detective hat? There's no such thing!" Mary scoffed.

"Oh, yes there is!" Harry replied. "Haven't you ever heard of Sherlock Holmes? He's the world's greatest detective! He wore a special kind of hat when he was trying to solve a case."

"That's true," ZuZu said. "I've seen pictures of Sherlock Holmes in a book. He is a famous character in lots of detective stories by Sir Arthur Conan Doyle. He wears a deerstalker hat. My dad tells me about some of his adventures."

"Cool!" Harry said. Then he reached into a brown bag and pulled out a baseball cap. "I'm about to show you my deerstalker hat. When I get it on, I'll be ready to investigate."

Mary rolled her eyes. "I think you'll be ready for baseball."

"I'm not done yet," Harry snapped.

We watched him reach into his bag again and take out a second baseball cap. He put the second one on top of the first so the visor was facing in the other direction.

ZuZu nodded slowly. "You know, Harry . . . that kind of looks like a deer-stalker hat now."

"It will be good for shade," Song Lee added.

Ida and Mary snickered and giggled.

Dexter and Sidney shook their heads.

"So what are you investigating, Harry?" ZuZu asked.

Harry took off both caps and hung them up on a hook. "Well, that's the problem, Zu. I don't have a case yet. But when I do, I'll be ready!"

Oh, boy, I thought. *I hope it's an easy one.* I didn't want Harry to botch up two cases in a row. His reputation as a detective was on the line!

As soon as we said the pledge and heard the morning announcements, we got a surprise visitor. It was Mrs. Funderburke, our school cook!

She was holding a blue plastic lunch tray with a carton of milk in the upper right-hand compartment. Harry flashed a toothy smile. He loves her. "Hi, Mrs. Funderburke!" he said. "What are you doing out of the kitchen?"

14

"Hi, Harry! Hi, boys and girls!"

"Hi, Mrs. Funderburke," the class replied.

"I'm coming around to make an exciting announcement to each classroom."

Lots of us leaned forward in our seats.

"I think we have the best students at South School," she said.

We all smiled.

Harry stood up and took a bow.

"So we are going to have some lucky lunch trays for February fun!"

"Lucky lunch trays?" we all replied.

Song Lee clasped her hands together.

Mary pretended to clap. She didn't want to make any noise.

"Starting today, one lucky person in each classroom will find an orange star sticker underneath their milk carton or juice box." She lifted her milk carton up and tilted the blue lunch tray so all of us could see.

"The star is pumpkin orange!" ZuZu said.

"It's big!" Ida said.

"It's sparkly!" Mary exclaimed.

"If you find one," Mrs. Funderburke continued, "bring it to me."

Then she set her tray down on a near-by desk and reached into her pocket.

"I will give you this!" she said, holding up a gold coin.

"Ooooh!" we said.

"One gold coin for your orange sticker," Mrs. Funderburke said. "It will buy you one treat from the Student Store!"

Now everyone clapped and cheered.

Harry put two thumbs up. "There's

one thing in that Student Store worth its weight in gold," he announced.

We all waited to hear Harry's choice. *"The light-up Wiffle Ball!"*

Dexter and I cheered. We thought it was cool too.

Mary pooh-poohed it. "I'd pick the pink princess notebook."

"I'd pick the monster eraser with the crazy blue hair," Sid chuckled.

"I know what I'd pick," Song Lee said softly. "My favorite thing." And then she didn't say what it was.

Mrs. Funderburke continued, "There will be lots of treasures to choose from in the Student Store. But," she added, "if your name was on the cafeteria chalkboard yesterday, your sticker won't be good today."

Sidney and Harry frowned.

Mary did another silent clap.

ZuZu raised his hand. "How are you going to decide which lunch tray gets an orange star? Will it be fair?"

Mrs. Funderburke picked up her stuff and headed for the door. "It will be very fair, ZuZu. I'm learning about a special set of numbers in a college math class I'm taking. It will give everyone a chance to win."

When I looked back at Harry, he wasn't frowning anymore. He had a smile as big as that Cheshire Cat in

Alice in Wonderland. Ear to ear!

"Why are you so happy, Harry?" I whispered.

"I just got a case!" he replied. "The biggest case ever in Room 3B! Who in our room will get a lucky lunch tray!"

"But that's impossible!" I said.

"Not for the world's second-best detective! Me! You heard Mrs. Funderburke," Harry explained. "She has a special set of numbers. All I have to do is figure out what it is, and bingo! Case solved!"

I covered my face with both hands.

Oh, no, I thought. This case had college math! It was not going to be lucky for Harry!

The Schnozzola

I was glad when Miss Mackle started science. It was Harry's favorite subject. I was hoping it might get his mind off his big detective case.

The teacher was holding a giant model of a human nose. "Boys and girls, we've been studying our five senses. This week we'll learn fascinating facts about the nose and how important our sense of smell is."

"I love the *schnozzola!*" Harry exclaimed.

Sidney cackled. "Yeah! The big schnozz!"

The teacher opened up the giant nose and showed us what it looked like way back in our nostrils.

"These little hairs are called *cilia*," she said. "They're like whisk brooms. They keep most of the dust and dirt from going down into our lungs. They're so small you can only see them with a microscope. The cilia appear bigger here."

22

"Cool!" ZuZu replied.

"I bet the dust and dirt makes good boogers," Harry said.

Mary cringed as Song Lee giggled.

"Actually, Harry," Miss Mackle answered, "you're right. Our nose mucus is like glue. It captures all that dust and dirt. So when we blow our nose, we get rid of . . ."

Suddenly Sidney sneezed into his hands.

"Sidney," the teacher said, "you just got rid of germs at about one hundred miles per hour!"

"Whoa!" I said.

"Can I go wash my hands?" Sid asked.

"Good idea," Miss Mackle replied.

When Sidney returned, the teacher explained our next activity. "You can do this by yourself or with a partner. Find something in our room that smells. Put it in a cup, tape paper over it, and punch a few holes on top. Later, we'll see if we can use our sense of smell to detect what the hidden object is."

Harry raised his hand.

"Yes?" the teacher said.

"May Doug and I go to the cafeteria? I want to ask Mrs. Funderburke if she could donate something that smells for our cup."

"How resourceful, Harry!" Miss Mackle replied. "Since it was your idea, you and Doug may go. But I'm not sending anyone else. Mrs. Funderburke is a very busy lady. Remember to ask her nicely, and thank her for her time."

"We will!" Harry said. "Come on, Doug!"

Mary blew up her bangs. She wanted to go too! On our way out, Harry grabbed his two baseball caps off the hook.

Now I knew what Harry was really up to! His schnozzola smelled a possible clue for his big detective case!

The First Clue

When Harry and I got to the cafeteria, Mrs. Funderburke was holding a vegetable steamer. It looked like a giant chrome castle to me.

"Just about done!" she said.

When a whiff drifted our way, I made a face. I didn't like the smell of broccoli.

Harry flashed a toothy smile. "Are you cooking my favorite vegetable?" he asked.

27

"I sure am!" Mrs. Funderburke replied. "Nice hat, Harry! What brings you boys to my kitchen?"

"A favor," Harry said. "We're studying the nose in Room 3B, and we need something that smells."

Mrs. Funderburke laughed. "You came to the right place. How about your favorite green vegetable, Harry? I can cut off one small floret for you."

"No, thank you," Harry replied.

"You want something with more aroma?" she asked with a smile.

"Yeah! Something that stinks!" Harry replied.

Mrs. Funderburke pointed to the menu on the wall. "Remember what we had last Friday?"

Harry patted his stomach. "I sure do! Mmm!"

"I do too," I groaned. "That's why I brought a cold lunch."

Mrs. Funderburke chuckled. "I've got a few portions left. You can take one."

"All right!" Harry exclaimed.

As soon as she walked over to the cafeteria refrigerator, Harry and I quickly sniffed around for clues.

The familiar blue plastic trays with six compartments were piled in stacks. The spork and napkin packets were packed in a bin.

I could see chicken nuggets and fries in the oven through the glass doors. They were on huge silver trays. I liked the smell of the chicken and potatoes cooking.

Harry waved me over to a small yellow bulletin board with pictures of a

sunflower, black-eyed Susans, broccoli, and cauliflower. Block letters spelled out two words, followed by numbers:

FIBONACCI SEQUENCE
1, 1, 2, 3, __, __, __,

Suddenly Mrs. Funderburke was standing next to us. "Here, Harry," she said, handing him a paper cup with tinfoil over it.

"Thanks a lot!" Harry said. Then he abruptly changed the subject. "What do the numbers on this bulletin board mean?"

Mrs. Funderburke smiled and said, "Oh, that! Mr. Fib-ba-notch-chee is going to help me place the orange stars on the lucky lunch trays. Run along now, boys!"

On our way back to class, Harry whipped out his small notebook and wrote down the numbers: 1, 1, 2, 3. "It's a code! Her special set of numbers!"

"Yeah!" I replied. "I wonder if today's winner will be number four—the fourth person in line. What do you think, Harry?"

"I'm thinking about that name, Fibonacci. I've heard it somewhere before."

Harry pulled the visor down on his detective hat. "I'm also thinking about those two ones in the beginning of the sequence. What do they mean?"

I shrugged. I didn't know.

"I have to see who the first winner is today, Doug. Then I might be able to figure out who will be the orange-star winner tomorrow!"

I was impressed.

Harry wasn't jumping to conclusions.

He was taking things slow.

He knew his reputation as a detective was at stake.

Payback Time!

The next half hour was fun. We got in small groups and tried to guess each other's mystery smells. Harry made sure he was in Mary's group. I knew why.

It was payback time for her tattling yesterday!

"Remember, boys and girls," the teacher said. "Smell the mystery item first, write down your answer in your science notebooks, and don't tell anyone. After each person has had a turn using their sense of smell, then read your answers out loud."

"How come you haven't poked any holes in the top?" I whispered to Harry.

"I will when the time comes. I want the smell to be really ripe," he explained.

"Okay," I whispered back. Harry was a pro when it came to gross smells.

"Someone else can go first," Harry said politely. "Doug and I want to be last."

Mary had her own paper cup. Four neat holes were punched on top. It was obvious she had used her hole puncher. "See if you can tell what it is, Doug," she said, passing it to me.

I took a whiff. It was sweet. I wrote a word down.

Song Lee took a whiff. "I like it!" she

said, then she wrote down her answer.

Harry took one whiff and said, "Piece of cake!"

"*Harry!*" Mary said. "You're not supposed to say your answer out loud. I'm telling!" Then she called out, "Miss Mackle!"

Uh-oh! Mary was tattling on Harry again.

The teacher came right over. When she found out what Harry said, she wasn't angry.

"'Piece of cake' is an expression, Mary. He thinks your smell is easy."

As soon as Miss Mackle left our group, Mary made fish lips and pouted.

The rest of us shared our answers. We all said "cake" except for Harry.

"It's frosting," he said.

Mary tilted her cup so we could see. It was pink frosting.

Harry threw his shoulders back and stood tall. "I got it!" he sang out. "I'm not just a private eye. I'm a private schnozz!"

Sidney and Song Lee laughed.

"Where did you get that frosting, Mary?" ZuZu asked. "I thought you were having hot lunch today."

Now Mary could brag. "I am," she said. "I'm just resourceful. I asked the teacher if I could take some frosting from that birthday cupcake she had on her desk. Remember, a second-grader brought it in for her?"

We all nodded.

We did a lot of smelling that morning. Harry and I guessed Song Lee and Ida's soap, ZuZu's cedar chips from our guinea pig JuJu's cage, and Dexter's chalk dust. We didn't get Sidney's eraser.

Finally, it was our turn.

"How come your paper cup doesn't have holes in it?" Mary snapped.

Harry reached for a pair of scissors, jabbed a hole in the foil, and then cut out a circle. "It does now!" He grinned.

"You're about to smell one of my favorite aromas. But"—he paused, holding up a finger—"you need to take a deep whiff. It's hard to pick up its scent. You may go first, Mary," Harry said.

Mary flared her nostrils a couple of times. Then she leaned over the cup and inhaled deeply.

"Aaaaaauuuuuuuugh! Fish! *Yuck!*"

Harry shook a finger. "Actually, it's pollack. We had it for lunch on Friday. And you're not supposed to shout out

your answer," he scolded. "You're supposed to write it down. So . . . I'm telling on you, Mare!"

Mary covered her mouth quickly. Her eyes bulged. She hid behind Song Lee.

"I told you your tattling would backfire on you sometime!" Harry snapped. "Well, it just did!"

Mary's body was shaking.

"How does it feel when someone's going to tattle on you?" Harry asked. "Huh?"

"N-n-not s-s-s-so g-g-g-good," Mary stuttered.

Harry got his payback, all right. And the weird thing was, he never did tattle to the teacher. He just let Mary suffer and think about being tattled on! And that was good enough for Harry.

The First Orange-Star Winner!

At lunchtime we all lined up to go to the cafeteria. Dexter was first, then ZuZu, Sidney, Ida, Song Lee, Mary, Harry, and me.

"Will the fourth person in line get the lucky lunch tray, Harry?" I whispered.

"I'm not so sure," Harry whispered back. "We'll just have to wait and see."

Mary had her fingers crossed as we snaked our line into the kitchen. Song

Lee was wearing a special charm necklace. "Pigs mean good luck in Korea," she said. "I hope they bring me good luck today."

Mrs. Funderburke had our stack of trays hidden behind a poster. Each time she reached for a tray, she plopped a milk carton or juice box on top before she moved it out to the counter where we were. No one could see if there was a sticker underneath.

As we scooted through the line, we could see the two cafeteria ladies with their plastic gloves helping Mrs. Funderburke. One aide dropped chicken nuggets in the middle compartment and a handful of French fries in another. She passed the lunch tray down to the next aide, who filled the remaining compartments with a serving of broccoli, a packet of carrots, and a packet with a spork and a napkin.

When Harry came through the line, the aide dishing out the broccoli said, "The usual, Harry?"

"Yes, please," he answered.

And she gave him two heaping servings.

As soon as we got to our table, we lifted our milk cartons to see who had an orange star.

"Boo!" Mary said. "I didn't get one!"

"I'm glad I didn't get one," Sidney said. "My name was on the board yesterday. It would have been wasted."

I checked underneath my milk. Nope.

Suddenly Song Lee sang out, "I have the lucky lunch tray! My pig necklace *was* good luck. I'm so happy I wore it today! See my orange star?" Harry and I looked at the star, then at each other.

Song Lee was not the third or fourth person in line. She was the *fifth* person in line. Song Lee peeled the orange sticker off her tray, jumped out of her seat, and hurried to the kitchen.

Harry and I went into deep thought.

The pattern of numbers Mrs. Funderburke was using was one, one, two, three, and now five!

While we all sat there feeling like losers, Mrs. Doshi stopped by our table with a big red bottle. "Who wants ketchup?" she asked. We watched her squirt some ketchup on Ida's plate. She didn't squirt it in one place—she made a ketchup happy face.

"Oh, that's so cute. Can I have one too?" Mary asked.

"Sure," Mrs. Doshi said. "You know how to use ketchup packets properly."

Mary beamed.

When Sidney asked for ketchup, Mrs. Doshi just gave him one glob. "Where's my happy face?" Sid complained.

Suddenly Mr. Skooghammer, our computer teacher, walked into the cafeteria. As he cut to the front of the line, Harry tapped Mrs. Doshi's arm.

"Excuse me, Mrs. Doshi," he said. "I need permission to talk to Mr. Skooghammer. It's about math. May I, please? It's really important."

Mrs. Doshi squeezed one glob of ketchup onto Harry's plate. "I'm glad you have better lunchtime manners today. Yes, you may, Harry. But be brief!"

"You're the best!" Harry replied. "I promise it will just be a one-minute conversation!" Then he dashed over to Mr. Skooghammer. He had a chef-salad plate in his hand and was nibbling on some celery. I watched him talk with Harry and nod and smile and laugh.

It was the longest one-minute conversation I've ever watched.

When Harry returned, I got the scoop.

"What did he say?" I whispered.

"Well," Harry said, dipping a sprig of broccoli in his ketchup, "I asked him if he remembered last June when he was the teacher in the Suspension Room. And he said yes. That was where he first met me."

I chuckled. That was funny. "Yeah?"

Harry continued, "I asked him if he remembered the cool lesson he taught me in math because I was a little fuzzy on it. And he said, 'You mean the Fibonacci sequence?' And I said, 'Yes.' And then he lit up like a Christmas tree and said, 'You remembered?' And then I said, 'Kind of.' I knew the sequence went one, one, two, three, five, but I didn't know the next number. And then Mr. Skooghammer gave me a super clue. He said just look at the last two numbers. When I did, I figured it out! I cracked the code!"

I couldn't. But if Harry could, that was a good thing. "All right!" I said, slapping him five.

Harry immediately tapped his tray with his spork. It didn't make a very loud noise, but he got the attention of kids close by. "I know who is going to get the lucky lunch tray tomorrow!" he announced.

"That's impossible!" Mary groaned.

"Not for the world's second-best detective," Harry replied.

"Who's the best detective?" Sid asked. "I forgot."

"*Sherlock Holmes!*" we replied.

"So," Mary said, "who does the world's second-best detective say the lucky lunch tray winner is tomorrow? Hmmm?"

Harry flashed a toothy smile. He liked his title.

"I don't have my detective hat on right now, Mare, so I can't tell you. But tomorrow when I come to school, I can."

Mary rolled her eyes.

I secretly crossed my fingers under the table.

The World's Second-Best Detective?

The next morning while we waited for Harry to come to school, we gathered around Song Lee. She was showing us what she got at the Student Store with her gold coin.

"Oooh!" Ida said. "A pen with a peacock feather at the end!"

"Show us how it works!" Mary said. "Please!"

Song Lee wrote seven words in her

notebook: I got a pretty rainbow pen today.

Each time she wrote a new word, she flicked the side of her pen and a new color of ink appeared.

"Look!" ZuZu said. "The words are in red, orange, yellow, green, blue, indigo, and violet. All seven colors of the rainbow!"

"Oooooh!" Mary and Ida said.

"I hope my horseshoe charm bracelet brings me luck today," Mary said, making it rattle. "I want the next gold

coin! I want to get a rainbow pen too!"

When I looked up at the clock, there was one minute to the bell. "Where's Harry?" I asked.

"I'll bet he doesn't show up!" Mary moaned. "He doesn't know who is going to get the lucky lunch tray today."

"You're right, Mare!" a voice sang out from the hall.

"It's Harry!" everyone said. He was wearing his detective hat.

Mary beamed. She loved being right.

"Well, actually, Mare," Harry continued, "you're half right. I don't know *who* will get the lucky lunch tray. But," he said, tapping his pocket, "I do know *where* a person has to stand in line to get it!"

We watched Harry reach into his

pocket. "After a lot of investigating, I found out Mrs. Funderburke is using the Fibonacci sequence. That's her special set of numbers."

"Fib-bone-not-shee?" Sidney repeated.

"Yup!" Harry replied. "He's the guy who discovered the code!"

"You know the lucky place where someone has to stand today?" ZuZu asked.

"I sure do!" Harry said, holding up a folded piece of paper. "Got it written down!"

"Then tell us now!" Mary demanded.

"Can't," Harry said, tucking his paper back into his pocket. "It would spoil the surprise."

"When will you tell us?" ZuZu asked.

"When everyone's in the lunch line,"

Harry said. "Just before we step into the kitchen."

"Awww," we groaned.

"Hey, I just solved a tough case with only two clues. You have to be patient for my solution," Harry said, hanging up his detective hat.

Mary folded her arms. "I bet I know which place it will be in line!" she said with a grin.

"We'll see!" Harry said, walking to his seat.

I was sure glad we did something fun in class that morning, because the minutes were ticking away like hours! We couldn't wait to find out the second winner!

Miss Mackle set up a science demonstration. "Boys and girls," she said, "I hope this experiment shows how important our sense of smell is when we taste something."

We watched the teacher as she stood behind a table with newspaper on it. "What do I have in this hand?"

"An apple," we said.

"And in this hand?"

"A potato," we replied.

"I will now peel each one," she said, reaching for a potato peeler.

We watched the red skin from the apple and the brown spotted skin from the potato fall to the table. When she finished, she asked a question. "Can you tell them apart?"

"No," we answered.

Miss Mackle set the apple on a paper plate and chopped it into small chunks. On another paper plate she did the same thing to the potato.

"Let's start with the first person in row one," she said.

Ida popped out of her seat.

Miss Mackle put a blindfold over her eyes to make sure she couldn't see what was on each plate. "Now, hold your nose, Ida," she said.

"I will," Ida replied. Her voice sounded nasal.

Everyone leaned forward in their chair.

"Taste this," the teacher said, giving her one small sample.

Ida held her nose and took a bite.

"Is it apple or potato?" Miss Mackle asked.

Ida shrugged. "I don't know. It just tastes crunchy."

"Taste it now without holding your nose," the teacher said.

Ida took her fingers away and tasted the sample. "It's an apple!"

"We need our schnozz to taste stuff?" Harry blurted out.

"We sure do!" Miss Mackle replied.

"Our sense of taste depends on our sense of smell. Next!"

By the time everyone got a turn, it was almost lunchtime.

We couldn't wait!

As soon as the bell rang, we lined up and hurried down to the cafeteria. Harry had his detective hat on.

"So who is in the lucky place, Harry?" ZuZu asked.

Mary answered before he could say one word.

"It has to be the sixth place because that's where Harry is standing!" Mary snapped. "If he knows what place in line is going to get the lucky lunch tray, he'll be standing in that place. Harry wants that light-up Wiffle Ball from the Student Store!"

"That's true," Harry said. "I do want

that Wiffle Ball, but I'm not standing in the lucky place." Harry took out a piece of paper from his pocket and read it. "The eighth person is!" he announced.

We turned around and quickly counted.

"*Sidney!*" everyone replied.

Sidney was clapping his hands and jumping up and down.

"Save your energy," Mary said. "Harry botched up his last case, remember?"

Sid stopped jumping and made a face.

One by one, Mrs. Funderburke handed us our blue lunch tray with a milk carton on it. A few people asked for juice instead. One by one, the cafeteria aides added a large square of pizza, a bag of carrot sticks, a plastic container of applesauce, a big chocolate chip cookie, and a packet with a spork and napkin.

When we got to our lunch table, I checked under my milk carton. The orange sticker wasn't there.

"Boo again!" Mary said. "I don't have it!"

"Me either," Ida said.

Mary lifted up Harry's milk carton. "He doesn't have it!"

"*I do!*" Sidney said, ripping it off his lunch tray. He held the orange star sticker high in his hand. "I'm getting a gold coin!"

"Well," Harry cooed. "Like I said, Sidney was the eighth person in line. What do you have to say, Mare?"

Mary slowly sank down in her chair. In a very soft voice she said, "You got it right this time."

We all clapped for Harry.

Harry took a bite of pizza and leaned back in his chair. He was feeling good!

"So, how come you didn't stand in the eighth place in line, Harry?" I whispered. "You could have gotten that gold coin."

"'Cause solving a tough case is the best prize of all," Harry said. "Cracking a code beats getting a light-up Wiffle Ball."

I nodded.

Harry wasn't just a real detective. He was a real winner.

A real winner doesn't need a prize.

Epilogue

Mrs. Funderburke used these Fibonacci numbers for her February fun: 5, 8, 13, 21. She was planning to make 1 her next number after 21.

But Mary's tattling changed that.

Mary waited three days before she tattled again. And when she did, it was to Mrs. Funderburke. "Harry knows your special set of numbers," Mary said. "He cracked the code. But he doesn't tell us until we're all lined up, and he never stands in the winning place."

Mrs. Funderburke said Harry was an honorable detective. But she would no longer use the Fibonacci numbers. She was just going to pick a number out of a jar.

Harry's reign as the world's second-best detective only lasted four days. But he loved every minute of it!

Who was Leonardo Fibonacci?

Leonardo Fibonacci was a famous Italian mathematician who lived from around 1175 to 1250. He recorded a unique sequence of numbers found in patterns in nature and musical chords: 1, 1, 2, 3, 5, 8, 13 . . .

How did Mr. Skooghammer teach Harry the Fibonacci numbers?

In the book *Horrible Harry and the*

Dungeon, Mr. Skooghammer taught Harry about the Fibonacci sequence. He showed Harry things from nature like pineapples and pinecones that illustrate this number pattern.

Starting with this sequence, you can figure out the rest of the pattern: 1, 1, 2, 3, 5, 8, 13, 21 . . .

You add the last two numbers and the sum is the next number. So one plus one is two, one plus two is three, two plus three is five, three plus five is eight, five plus eight is thirteen, and eight plus thirteen is twenty-one!

Can you guess which number comes next?

Can you write the Fibonacci numbers up to almost one thousand?

(Go to www.suzykline.com to find out the answer!)